JACK RUSSELL:
Dog Detective

The Lying
Postman

JACK RUSSELL: Dog Detective

JACK RUSSELL:
Dog Detective

The Lying
Postman

DARREL & SALLY ODGERS

Kane Miller
A DIVISION OF EDC PUBLISHING

First American Edition 2007
by Kane/Miller Book Publishers, Inc.
La Jolla, California

First published by Scholastic Press in 2005

For information contact:
Kane Miller, A Division of EDC Publishing
P.O. Box 470663
Tulsa, OK 74147-0663
www.kanemiller.com
www.edcpub.com
www.usbornebooksandmore.com

Library of Congress Control Number: 2006931566
Printed and bound in the United States of America
7 8 9 10 11 12 13 14 15
ISBN: 978-1-933605-31-9

Dear Readers,

The story you're about to read is about me and my friends, and how we solved the case of The Lying Postman. To save time, I'll introduce us all to you now. Of course, if you know us already, you can trot off to the first chapter.

I am Jack Russell, Dog Detective. I live with my landlord, Sarge, in Doggeroo. Sarge detects human-type crimes. I detect the crimes that deal with dogs. I'm a Jack Russell terrier, so I am dogged and intelligent.

Next door to Sarge and me live Auntie Tidge and Foxie. Auntie Tidge is lovely. She has biscuits. Foxie is not lovely. He's a fox terrier (more or less).

He used to be a street dog, and a thief, but he's reformed now. Auntie Tidge has even got rid of his fleas. Foxie sometimes helps me with my cases.

Uptown Lord Setter (Lord Red for short) lives in Uptown House with Caterina Smith. Lord Red means well, but he isn't very bright.

We have other friends and acquaintances in Doggeroo. These include Polly the dachshund, Jill Russell, the Squekes and Shuffle the pug. Then there's Fat Molly Cat from the library.

That's all you need to know, so let's get on with the first chapter.

Yours doggedly,

Jack Russell – the detective with a nose for crime.

The Yowling Basket

Foxie and I were digging a hole in Foxie's yard. Kitty Booker, the Doggeroo librarian, came through the gate, carrying a big basket.

"I smell food," said Foxie, and started to drool. Foxie will eat anything he can get.

I made a quick **nose map**.

Jack's map:

1. The beef bone Foxie had
   hidden under a bush.

2. The **special biscuits** Auntie
   Tidge makes.

3. Foxie's old boot.

4. Cat food.

5. Cat.

"It's Cat Crunchies," I said. "It's also Fat Molly."

Foxie bristled. "Where? Where?"

I sniff-sniffed the air. "She's in that basket with the Cat Crunchies," I said.

As Kitty Booker walked past us, Foxie growled at the basket.

The basket yowled back.

Jack's Facts

Baskets don't yowl.
Cats yowl.
So, baskets that yowl must have a cat inside.
This is a fact.

Foxie growled at the basket again. No terrier can see a basket full of cat in his **terrier-tory** and not take action. Before he could do anything about it, Auntie Tidge opened the door.

"Hello, Kitty!" said Auntie Tidge. "It *will* be nice to have Molly to stay!"

Kitty Booker held out the yowling basket. "Thanks, **Miss Russell**. It's really kind of you to look after Molly while I go to the conference. Tina Boxer usually looks after her, but now that she has her new dog, Ralf, she can't."

"It's no trouble at all," said Auntie Tidge.

Foxie growled, "It's going to be trouble for *me*." He glared at Kitty Booker and Auntie Tidge as she carried the basket into the house.

"Cheer up, Foxie," I said. "You can play **Cat-ch Cat**."

"**Dogwash**!" snapped Foxie. "Auntie Tidge won't let me!"

Jack's Facts

Where there are cats, there is cat food.
Cat food is good – even for dogs.
Dogs eat faster than cats.
This is a fact.

I reminded Foxie of this fact, and that cheered him up.

"I'm going to hide my old boot," he said. "And I'll bury my beef bone. And she's not sitting on my blanket. And she can't have any special biscuits."

"Cats don't eat special biscuits," I said. "They have their own tasty cat biscuits. It'll be all right. You'll see."

Just then, Sarge came home, so I scooted back into my own terrier-tory to **greet** him. Sarge is my landlord, and I don't want him to feel neglected.

Jack's Glossary

Nose map. *A way of storing information with the nose.*

Special biscuits. *Biscuits Auntie Tidge makes. They don't harm terrier teeth.*

Terrier-tory. *A territory owned by a terrier.*

Miss Russell. *I am Jack Russell. Sarge is Sergeant Russell. Auntie Tidge is Miss Russell.*

Jack's Glossary

Cat-ch Cat. *A game dogs play with cats.*

Dogwash. *Nonsense.*

Greet. *This is done by rising to the hind legs and clutching a person with the paws while slurping them up the face.*

# The Postman Game

Next morning, I was giving my breakfast bowl a good polish with my tongue when Foxie dragged his old boot into my yard.

"You haven't been eating cat food, have you?" I asked. (My **super-sniffer** told me that he hadn't.)

Foxie dropped the boot. "I haven't had breakfast, either."

"That's pawful!" I said. "You're not sick are you? You're not dying?"

"It's Fat Molly's fault," grumbled Foxie. "Kitty Booker has her on a diet."

"What's that got to do with you?"

"Auntie Tidge has put *me* on a diet too!" snapped Foxie. "She won't give me special biscuits until I lose weight!"

Fat Molly came **pussyfooting** into my yard, waving her crooked tail. She sat down to lick herself.

Of course, I **jack-yapped** at her. "Scat cat!" I yapped. "Scat, fat cat!"

Fat Molly glared at me with her green eyes, and flicked a ragged ear. She said something **terrier-ably** rude, with spits in it. Then she rolled on Foxie's old boot.

Foxie snarled.

Fat Molly **cat-apulted** to her feet and jumped onto the gatepost.

Foxie jumped up and down, barking insults.

Jack's Facts

Cats insult dogs.
Dogs insult cats.
The cats always start it, therefore it's
their fault.
This is a fact.

"Foxie-woxie? What's going on?"
Auntie Tidge came bustling into my yard.

Jack's Facts

Humans always arrive after a cat
has been insulting.
Humans always arrive when a dog is
reacting.
Therefore, dogs get the blame.
This is a fact.

I **jack-jumped** into Auntie Tidge's
arms. I gave her a good swipe up the
face with my tongue and knocked her
glasses sideways. She loves it when I do
that.

Foxie glared at his boot. "Mine, mine,
mine!" he growled. "Mine, mine, mine."

"Foxie-woxie, no one wants your
boot." Auntie Tidge put me down and
picked up the boot. Foxie snatched it,

and dragged it under a bush. "Mine, mine, mine."

I stared. Foxie has always been **paw-ssessive** about that boot, but being on a diet was making him worse.

Auntie Tidge saw Fat Molly sitting on the gate. "Poor Molly-wollie. Has naughty Foxie been rude to you?"

Molly meowed sadly. Auntie Tidge dragged Foxie and the boot from under the bush. She dropped them both over the little hedge. Then she took Fat Molly and went home.

I chewed my **squeaker bone** for a while. I could still hear Foxie on the other side of the hedge muttering, "Mine, mine, mine."

"Let's play the Postman Game," I suggested.

The postman was coming up the street. Any minute, he'd rattle the mailbox.

Jack's Facts

Postmen always rattle mailboxes.
Dogs bark when postmen rattle.
Postmen yell when dogs bark.
That's how you play the Postman Game.
This is a fact.

We'd been playing that game with our postman for ages, but that day something went wrong.

Foxie barked. The postman yelled. Foxie barked some more.

The postman should then ride to my gate. I would bark and the postman would yell at me. But this postman didn't play. Instead, he opened Foxie's gate and kicked Foxie. The postman wasn't *our* postman. It was a new one.

Foxie yelped with shock and ran to hide under Auntie Tidge's bed.

I didn't know it yet, but that was the start of ... The Case of the Lying Postman.

Jack's Glossary

Super-sniffer. *Jack's nose in super-tracking mode.*

Pussyfooting. *The way cats walk. Also known as "catfooting."*

Jack-yap. *A loud, piercing yap made by a Jack Russell terrier.*

Terrier-ably. *Very.*

Cat-apult. *A very fast movement made by a cat when a terrier is barking at it.*

Jack's Glossary

Jack-jump. *A sudden spring made by a Jack Russell terrier.*

Paw-ssessive. *The way some dogs get when someone tries to take away their belongings.*

squeaker bone. *Something for exercising a terrier's jaws. Not to be confused with a toy.*

 The Lying Postman

When Foxie raced inside, Auntie Tidge came out. "Whatever's going on?"

"Your dog tried to bite me," the postman lied.

"That's a lie!" I jack-yapped.

Foxie's manners are **terrier-able**, but biting isn't part of the Postman Game.

"Foxie can't get out if the gate's shut," Auntie Tidge said. "So he *could not* have bitten you."

Jack's Facts

Terriers jump over.
Terriers burrow under.
Terriers push through.
Auntie Tidge doesn't know everything.
This is a fact.

"Did you open the gate?" Auntie Tidge asked.

"No!" snapped the postman. "That dog jumped up and tried to bite me."

"That's a lie!" I jack-yapped again. I jack-jumped a few times.

"That mongrel is trying to bite me, too," said the postman, pointing at me.

"Nonsense," said Auntie Tidge. "Jack's just curious."

The postman grumbled past my

gate. I didn't bark again. He didn't play fair, and he didn't even know what kind of dog I was. He thought I was a *mongrel*!

Auntie Tidge thought he was stupid too. She shook her head and went off to do her shopping.

I put my chin on my paws. There was **skulldoggery** afoot. I could smell it in the air.

"Jack Russell's the name, detection's the game," I said aloud, but how could I investigate this crime? There was nothing *to* investigate. I sat down to look at the facts.

1. The Crimes: kicking Foxie; lying to Auntie Tidge.
2. The **Pupetrator**: the postman.
3. The Method: kicking and lying.
4. The Opportunity: the postman had been passing our gates.
5. Possible Motive: hatred of dogs.

It all seemed clear to me. There was nothing *to* investigate.

The Case of the Lying Postman seemed dead in the water.

When Auntie Tidge had gone, Foxie slunk out of the house. My super-sniffer detected him on the other side of the hedge. He was muttering, "It's not fair. It's not fair. It's not fair."

"**Ig-gnaw** that Lying Postman, Foxie."

"You're not the one that got kicked,"

said Foxie. "You're not the one forced to go on a diet." Foxie's belly rumbled.

Fat Molly hopped on to the end of the fence and called Foxie something terrier-able, but he ig-gnawed her.

"I'd offer you some of my breakfast if I hadn't already eaten it," I said. "At least you'll get a good supper."

Foxie did get supper, but he wasn't **pawfully** pleased with it.

"Auntie Tidge gave me *carrots*," he snarled. "What does she think I am – a rabbit?"

"Carrots?" I was shocked. The thought of a rabbit that looked like Foxie was truly **terrier-fying**.

"Carrots and Cat Crunchies," moaned Foxie. His belly rattled again. "Fat Molly got Cat Crunchies too. Auntie

Tidge fed her on top of the fridge."

That was mean of Auntie Tidge. How is a terrier expected to get his teeth on a cat's food if the cat is fed on top of the fridge?

<u>Jack's Facts</u>

Good dogs don't steal from people.
Good dogs don't steal from dogs.
Taking food from cats isn't stealing.
This is a fact.

"I'd offer you some of my supper, but I already ate it," I said.

Being on a diet and having Fat Molly to stay had a terrier-able effect on Foxie's temper. Then being kicked by the Lying Postman was the **last paw**. Foxie said he was going to get revenge.

"Revenge on whom?" I asked

"Revenge on *everybody*," Foxie growled.

Jack's Glossary

Terrier-able. *Very bad.*

Skulldoggery. *Bad things concerning dogs.*

Pupetrator. *A criminal who does things to dogs.*

Ig-gnaw. *Ignore, but done by dogs.*

Pawfully. *Very, awfully.*

Terrier-fying. *Frightening.*

Last paw. *Like the last straw, but happening to dogs.*

Foxie's Revenge

When Foxie said everybody, he meant *everybody*. He even snarled at Auntie Tidge.

I was shocked. "Don't you snarl at Auntie Tidge!" I said.

"All right," said Foxie. "I'll ig-gnaw her instead."

That shocked me even more.

Foxie got his revenge on Fat Molly. He **terrier-ized** her by walking slowly up to her and muttering under his breath. Every time Fat Molly appeared, Foxie stalked her like this.

Jack's Facts

Cats are expert stalkers.
Dogs hate being stalked by cats.
Cats hate being stalked by dogs even
more.
This is a fact.

"Stop that, Foxie," I said. "Stalking will make you even hungrier."

Foxie ig-gnawed me. That was his revenge on me.

"I haven't done anything to you!" I said.

Foxie went and squatted over his old boot. In a few minutes I heard him muttering, "You'd think a greedy Jack would share his breakfast with a hungry pal."

I *would* have shared my breakfast with Foxie if I hadn't been hungry myself. When Auntie Tidge had stopped giving Foxie special biscuits, she stopped giving them to me, too!

Foxie got his revenge on the Lying Postman. He lurked behind the gate and yapped and snapped when the postman rattled the mailbox.

The postman threw Auntie Tidge's letters over the gate.

"That dog next door is savage," he said to Sarge, who was just on his way to work.

Sarge laughed. "Savage?" He raised his voice over Foxie's yapping. "Foxie isn't savage."

"It is savage," lied the Lying Postman. "It should be tied up."

"But he's in a secure yard," said Sarge.

"It should be tied up. I've already been bitten by one dog in this town. That one next door tried it too. If you don't do something about it, I'll call Ranger Jack."

While the Lying Postman was lying to Sarge, I made a quick nose map.

29

Jack's Map:

1. Empty breakfast bowl.

2. Foxie's old boot.

3. Fat Molly.

4. The Lying Postman.

5. Sarge.

6. Lord Red.

Lord Red? Because Foxie was ig-gnawing me, I needed company. Lord Red might have more hair than brains, but he's still a pal. I jack-jumped to look over the gate.

The Lying Postman sprang backwards. "That mongrel should be tied up too!" he said, pointing at me.

"Jack is only looking over the gate," explained Sarge. "Now, can you describe the dog that you claim *did* bite you? If it's running loose, Ranger Jack will take it to the pound."

"How should I know what sort of dog it was? I tell you, it bit me! Look!"

The Lying Postman showed a rip in his uniform jacket. "You can see the marks."

"Nasty rip you have there," agreed Sarge. "I need details about the dog. Drop in to the station later and give me the facts."

The Lying Postman gave me a nasty look. He called me a terrier-able name and pedaled away.

Jack's Glossary

Terrier-ize. *To frighten, done by a terrier.*

# Red is Upsettered

I jack-jumped again to make sure the Lying Postman had gone. Lord Red was prancing up the street towards him like a hairy shampoo model.

As Red passed the Lying Postman, the postman's bike swerved. Red yelped, spun round and tore off back the way he'd come.

"Red!" I called. "Halt in the name of the paw!"

Red kept on running, so I left the yard (never mind how) and ran after him.

I needed to find out what had **upsettered** him.

We ran past Dora Barkins' house. The three Squekes were yaffling in their yard. We ran past the library and up to the showground. I caught Red on the hill. He didn't stop when I jack-yapped, so I jack-jumped and grabbed his tail in my teeth.

"Ow-wow-wowwwww!" howled Red. He spun round three times, so fast my **jack-jaws** lost their grip. He sat down and put his paw on his tail.

After *that*, he spotted me. "Jack? Where did you come from, Jack? Jack, I just had a horrible thing happen. Something grabbed my tail! I think it was a **dognapper**. Will you take the case, Jack? Will you?"

My ears had turned inside out when I lost my grip, so I shook them the right way out.

"Calm down, Red," I ordered.

"A dognapper grabbed my tail!" repeated Red.

"That was me," I said. "I had to stop you."

Red jumped up, but he had his paw on his own tail, so he sat down again. "Why are you trying to dognap me, Jack?"

I groaned.

"*Nobody* is trying to dognap you," I said.

"Are you sure?" asked Red.

"Quite sure," I said. "Red, I need to ask you something."

"Are you going to **in-terrier-gate** me, Jack? Are you on a case?"

"Yes," I said. "The Case of the Lying Postman. Why were you running up our street?"

"I wanted to see you, Jack," said Red. "You're my best friend."

"Then why did you run back *down* our street instead of coming to my gate?"

"The dognapper on the bike rode at me," said Red. "It upsettered me, so I was running back to Caterina Smith. Caterina Smith says I mustn't let dognappers get me."

"For the last time, Red, *no one* is trying to dognap you!"

"Okay," said Red. "Why did the dognapper ride his bike at me, then?"

"He's not a dognapper. He's a postman," I said.

Red looked confused. "Postmen

don't chase dogs, Jack. Dogs chase postmen."

"This postman hates dogs," I said. "He's been telling lies about Foxie and me."

"But that's pawful!" said Red.

"Exactly," I said. "He's a lying postman. Telling lies is what liars do."

"Foxie lies," said Red. "He tells Auntie Tidge he hasn't been fed when he *has*."

Jack's Facts

Dogs are hunters.
Telling their people they haven't been fed is just another form of hunting.
Therefore lying about food isn't really lying.
This is a fact.

I explained this to Red.

"Oh," said Red. "I'm going hunting then." He jumped up and started galloping up the hill.

"Red!" I jack-yapped, but Red had gone.

Jack's Glossary

Upsettered. *Bothered and upset a setter.*

Jack-jaws. *The splendid set of jaws owned by a Jack Russell.*

Dognapper. *Someone who steals dogs.*

In-terrier-gate. *Official questioning, done by a terrier.*

 Paw-Leash Work

Since Red had **desettered** me, I had to
find someone else to in-terrier-gate.
This meant heavy **paw-leash** work.
But because Foxie was ig-gnawing me,
I had no one to help me.

   I started by going down to the
reserve to in-terrier-gate Shuffle the
pug, who lives with Walter Barkly. I
trotted up to Shuffle's yard and asked
pawmission to enter his territory.

Jack's Facts

Polite dogs always ask pawmission before entering someone else's territory.
It is especially polite if the dog is larger than the polite dog.
This has nothing to do with being afraid of larger dogs.
This is a fact.

Shuffle didn't know anything about postmen. Walter Barkly always collects his letters from the post office.

"Do you know who might have bitten the postman?" I asked.

"Foxie," said Shuffle. "He threatened to bite *me* once. I was terrier-ized."

"That was because you sat on his old boot," I said.

I left Shuffle and went over the river to visit Polly the dachshund, who lives with Gloria Smote. Polly was **daching** around with Jill Russell, who lives with Jack and Jill Johnson near the station.

I put my nose through Polly's gate. "What do *you* want, Jack?" she asked.

"I'm on a case," I explained. "There's a lying postman at large. He said Foxie bit him. Foxie didn't. He said I tried to bite him. I didn't. He rode his bike at Red and upsettered him. He said another dog bit him. It didn't. He – "

"How do you *know* it didn't?" demanded Jill Russell. She poked me with her nose. She always does that.

"Because he's a lying postman!" I said.

"Even lying postmen don't lie about everything," said Jill.

Time to get down to business, I thought. "Answer in the name of the paw," I said. "Did either of *you* bite the Lying Postman?"

"Of paws not!" snapped Polly. "The only thing *I* bite is the food Gloria Smote gives me."

"What about you, Jill Russell?" I continued doggedly.

Jill Russell told me to go and play with Ralf Boxer. "He's just your type," she said.

Boxer! That gave me paws for thought. Where had I heard that name before? I couldn't remember, so I headed off to in-terrier-gate the Squekes.

I might as well have saved my time. The Squekes were squeking around in Dora Barkins' yard as usual, yaffling and nipping one another.

"Did one of you Squekes bite the Lying Postman?" I demanded.

The Squekes yaffled at me. They flashed their fangs and shivered their long tails and hairy ears. It couldn't have been one of them that had bitten the postman. He said that only *one* dog had bitten him. The Squekes operate as a team. Either all three had bitten him or none of them had. Besides, I've never been absolutely sure that Squekes are dogs. They smell like dogs, but maybe they're really **dogbots**.

I went doggedly on around Doggeroo. None of the dogs I in-terrier-gated had bitten the Lying Postman, although some of them said he had lied and said they'd tried. I didn't meet any boxers, so finally, I went home.

Nothing had changed. Foxie was still ig-gnawing me. Auntie Tidge still wasn't making special biscuits. Sarge was still away. Fat Molly was licking herself on the gate.

Then I remembered where I'd heard Ralf Boxer's name before. Kitty Booker had said that Fat Molly couldn't stay with Tina Boxer because of her new dog, Ralf.

So, what did I know about Ralf Boxer?

1. He was a dog.
2. He was the reason Fat Molly couldn't stay with Tina Boxer.
3. He was probably a boxer.
4. Kitty Booker knew him.
5. Jill Russell said he was "just my type."

That wasn't enough for me to make an arrest. If I started in-terrier-gating Fat Molly, she'd probably cat-apult onto the roof and start **cat-erwauling**. Then Auntie Tidge would blame me.

Instead, I went back towards Uptown House to ask Red about Ralf

Boxer. Red is not the brightest biscuit in the box, but he goes everywhere and knows everyone.

Jack's Glossary

Desettered. *Desertion, done by a setter.*

Paw-leash work. *Detection done by a dog detective.*

Pawmission. *Permission, given by a dog.*

Jack's Glossary

Daching. *The way dachshunds get around.*

Dogbots. *Robotic dogs.*

Cat-erwauling. *A horrible noise made by a cat.*

 Red Alert

I trotted back past my house and
Foxie's place, turned right where the
three Squekes live, and crossed the
overpass. Then I ran into trouble.
Ranger Jack was on the prowl.

Don't ask me why Doggeroo Dog
Control Officer Johnny Wolf calls
himself *Ranger Jack*. Maybe he thinks
it's a snappy name.

Ranger Jack was talking to
someone, and I stopped to make a
nose map.

Jack's Map:

1. A corn dog
   wrapper someone
   had dropped.

2. Half a sausage roll.

3. A biscuit.

My belly rumbled. Detecting was making me hungry. I needed a biscuit break.

Sniff-sniff. Sniff-sniff. I started sneaking towards the source of the biscuit scent.

Sniff-sniff. Sniff- Oops! Now I smelled something else, mixed with the biscuits.

4. Ranger Jack.

5. The Lying Postman.

I jack-yapped with surprise. Big mistake.

"That's the mongrel that tried to bite me!" yelled the Lying Postman. "Just after the other mongrel tried to bite me and before the big red dog attacked me! Nearly had me off my bike."

"That's Sergeant Russell's Jack," said Ranger Jack.

"He said it never left the yard!" sneered the Lying Postman.

"That's a lie!" I jack-yapped.

"The dogs of Doggeroo are out of control," said the Lying Postman. "I demand you *do* something."

Ranger Jack sighed. "I'll speak to Caterina Smith. She's got the only big red dog I know, but Red wouldn't attack anyone. You're right about something, though. The dogs shouldn't be running around loose." He pulled a biscuit out of his pocket and held it out. "Hi, Jack … Come on, boy."

I was glad Foxie wasn't with me.

Foxie is anyone's for a biscuit, but Jack Russells are made of sterner stuff.

I jack-yapped again, dodged Ranger Jack, and ran to Uptown House.

I shot under Lord Red's hedge. "Red alert! Red alert! Hide!" I jack-yapped.

Jack's Facts

Polite dogs always ask pawmission before entering someone else's territory.
It is especially polite if the dog is larger than the polite dog.
In an emergency, even a polite dog might ig-gnaw this rule.
This is a fact.

Lord Red had been racing around, as usual. He skidded to a stop. His tail was whirling around like a propeller.

"Are we playing hide-the-Jack? Are we? Are weeeee?"

"Red alert!" I panted. "The Lying Postman is blackening your name. He told Ranger Jack you attacked him!"

"I didn't, Jack. I didn't! I wouldn't!" Red yelped. "Caterina Smith says dogs that attack get sent to the pouuunnnnd!"

"Be quiet!" I yapped. "They're coming."

Red and I burrowed under a bush, just before Ranger Jack and the Lying Postman knocked on the front door.

Caterina Smith opened the door. "Hello, Ranger Jack. Is there a problem?"

"Caterina, I'm sorry to tell you this, but the postman reckons a red setter and a Jack Russell attacked him. You

have a setter, and we saw Sarge's Jack
heading this way."

Caterina Smith laughed. "Lordie
doesn't attack people. He's here, but I
haven't seen Jack."

"Make sure your dog *is* here, please,"
said Ranger Jack.

"Of course." Caterina Smith called, "Lordie, *Lordie*! Lordieeeeee!"

Red quivered, but I had my jack-jaws on his tail. "Red! We're hiding!"

"But Caterina Smith is calling!" whined Red.

I had to act fast. "Red, do you know a dog called Ralf Boxer?"

"Of paws!" said Red. "He lives in the old-house-that-used-to-have-rats."

"Now we have a lead," I said. "If Ralf Boxer is the one who bit the Lying Postman, this is all his fault."

Red Herring

Red and I sneaked out of Red's garden and ran to the old-house-that-used-to-have-rats. I made a quick nose map.

Jack's Map:

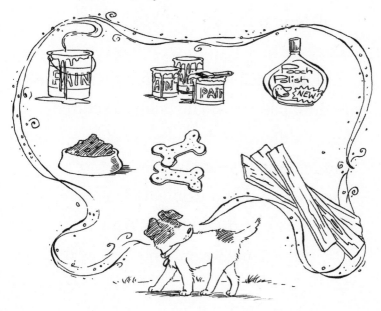

1. Paint.

2. More paint.

3. Pooch Polish.

4. Dog food.

5. Biscuits.

6. New timber.

It *did* smell different from the way it used to. I sneezed. The paint upset my super-sniffer, but there wasn't even a hint of a rat. It looked different, too. There was a brand new wooden fence. A person was painting the porch.

"That's Tina Boxer," said Red, as the

person went into the house. He got up on his hind legs and rested his front paws on the top of the new fence. He stuck his long nose over and sniffed. "I like Tina Boxer. She has biscuits." He began to edge along towards the biscuit-smell.

"Where – " I began, but before I got my question out, Red suddenly yelped and desettered me.

"My paw! My paw! My poor gnawed paw!" I heard him howling as he hopped away on three paws, carrying his left front one in the air.

"Red!" I jack-yapped, but Red was out of sight. I had a suspect to in-terrier-gate. And now it looked as if the suspect had bitten Red's paw.

I sniff-sniffed. The Lying Postman had been here, but not today. That made

sense if Ralf Boxer had really bitten him.
I hoped Ralf Boxer wasn't too big. Jack
Russells are scared of nothing, but it's
pawfully stupid to look for trouble.

Jack's Facts

Jack Russells are not big dogs.
They are exactly the right size.
Therefore, any dog bigger than a Jack
Russell is too big.
This is a fact.

I knew my way around the old-
house-that-had-had-rats, from when I
solved the Dog Den Mystery. The old
house was now Ralf Boxer's territory.
I could order Ralf Boxer to report for
in-terrier-gation, but what if he ig-gnawed

me? What if he gnawed *my* paw? Or even gnawed *me*?

I sniff-sniffed, to see if I could detect Ralf Boxer. He couldn't be far away, since he'd just bitten Red.

"Ralf Boxer?" I called politely. I put my nose under the fence. There was only a small gap, just enough for my jack-jaws and super-sniffer to fit through. "Ralf Boxer?" I repeated. "Are you there?"

I set my super-sniffer to work.

I *sniff-sniffed* right along the fence, but I couldn't smell a big dog.

And that wasn't all. If Ralf Boxer really lived here, why didn't he challenge me? Why didn't he threaten to rip my legs off and use them as toothpicks? Could Ralf Boxer be a terrier-able *coward*?

But wait. He *had* bitten Red, just for

putting his paws on the fence.

I had sniff-sniffed all the way along the fence and back again. I decided to try a few jack-jumps.

I bounced up like a **Jack-in-the-box**.

I was at the top of my jump when the smallest dog I've ever seen came out through the **dogdoor**. It was smaller than the rats that used to live in there. It would have fit into Sarge's breakfast cup.

It spotted me at the top of my jack-jump and came skittering over to the fence, yapping loudly.

"Be off, Big Dog! Be off! This is *my* **chihuahua-tory**!"

I tried not to laugh. Small dogs don't like to be laughed at by big dogs, and this was a *very* small dog. To this small dog, I was a big dog!

I pushed my nose into the gap under the fence. "Hi, pup. Does Ralf Boxer live here?"

"I am Ralf Boxer," said the small dog. "And *don't* call me 'pup'!"

"You can't be Ralf Boxer!"

"Why can't I?" A pointy little nose the size of a cherry pit jammed itself against mine and sniff-sniffed.

"Because you're not a boxer."

"Why would I be a boxer?"

"Then why are you called Ralf Boxer?"

"That's my name, not what I am. I mean, you're not called Jack Russell, are you?"

"Jack Russell's the name, detection's the game," I said.

"Oh." Ralf Boxer stared at me. "I'm coming out. Wait there."

Jack's Glossary

Jack-in-the-box. *A Jack in jumping-jack mode.*

Dogdoor. *A door especially for dogs.*

Chihuahua-tory. *A territory owned by a chihuahua.*

In-terrier-gation

Ralf Boxer crawled under the gate. He looked like a half-grown rat. His hair was so fine I could see the skin underneath. He was trying to raise his hackles.

Jack's Facts

Most dogs have hackles.
Some dogs have hackles that make other dogs laugh.
Dogs like that should not raise their hackles.
This is a fact.

"What do you want, Jack?" he yipped.

"Do you know Lord Red?" I asked.

"Of paws. He came with Caterina
Smith to have coffee with Tina Boxer.
He's silly. He thought I was a mouse."

"Is that why you bit him?"

Ralf goggled at me. "I didn't. Why

would I want to bite Lord Red? He's covered with hair!"

"Didn't you bite his paw just now when he put it over the fence?"

Ralf gave me a sarcastic look. "How would I do that, Jack?"

I looked at the fence. "Maybe you jumped up?"

Ralf Boxer sniffed. "Look, Jack. You are four times as tall as me. Even you can't jump as high as my fence."

"So, you *didn't* bite Lord Red just now," I **pawsisted**.

"I didn't know Lord Red was here."

"He isn't," I said.

Ralf gave me a funny look. "Have you been eating bad fish, Jack? You don't seem quite right in the head. First you say – "

"Stop!" I ordered. "Lord Red *was* here. Something bit his paw and he ran home. I thought it was you. Because I thought you were the dog that bit the Lying Postman. Since you can't be that dog, I'll be off. Thank you for helping with my enquiries."

"I *am* the dog that bit the postman," said Ralf.

"I quite understand. You — you *what?*"

"I did bite the postman," said Ralf. "He called me a nasty little brat and tried to kick me, so I bit him."

I was terrier-ably impressed. Ralf Boxer was the smallest dog I'd ever seen, and he'd started all this fuss!

"You do realize the Lying Postman is telling lies about the dogs in Doggeroo because of you?" I asked. "He thinks we're all out to get him. That means he's out to get us."

Ralf giggled.

"It's not funny!" I snapped. "Ranger Jack is after us." Then I remembered something. "How did you reach to bite the postman's jacket?"

"I didn't," said Ralf. "I bit his boot."

"You bit his boot?"

Ralf Boxer bristled. "What do you expect, Jack? I'm a chihuahua, not a bonehead."

My head was spinning. "Listen," I said. "One: the Lying Postman said Foxie and I tried to bite him. We didn't. Two: he said Lord Red attacked him. He didn't. Three: he said a dog bit him. You did. Four: the Lying Postman had been bitten in the middle. Five: you said you'd bitten the postman on the boot. And six: Lord Red said someone had bitten his paw. I thought it was you. But it wasn't."

"Is that all?" asked Ralf.

"No," I said. "Jill Russell said you were my kind of dog, and you're not."

"Are you intelligent, loyal, lively and brilliant in every way?" demanded Ralf Boxer.

"Yes," I said.

"Then I'm your kind of dog."

"But Kitty Booker said Tina Boxer couldn't look after Fat Molly because of you!"

Ralf Boxer had been looking pleased with himself, but now his eyes bugged out with terror. "Did you say *Fat Molly*? I *hate* Fat Molly! Fat Molly wants to *eat* me!" He was quivering like a cupful of jelly.

"Fat Molly couldn't stay here because *she* would attack *you?*" I asked. "I thought it was the other way round. Maybe some other things are the other way round too. *You* say you bit the Lying Postman on the boot. *He* says he was bitten in the jacket. You say you didn't bite Red at all. Red said his paw was bitten … and that means …"

"It means someone else must have bitten Lord Red *and* the Lying Postman's jacket," said Ralf Boxer.

"Or some *thing* else," I said.

I was about to continue the in-terrier-gation when Ralf Boxer looked past me and yelped. He dove back under the gate and vanished.

Ranger Jack and Sarge were coming around the corner with the Lying Postman.

"Jack? What are *you* doing here?" demanded Sarge.

"I told you so! This dog is *not* in its yard," said the Lying Postman, and pounced on me.

Jack's Glossary

Pawsisted. *Kept doggedly on.*

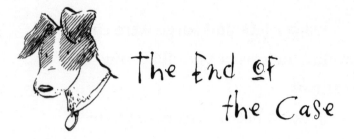

The End of the Case

There's only one thing to do when you're caught red-pawed out of your yard, and that's to practice **jack-straction**.

I jack-yapped and jack-jumped as hard as I could.

The Lying Postman had to let me go. I sailed over the fence and landed inside the yard.

"Get out of my chihuahua-tory, Jack!" yapped Ralf Boxer, and bit me on the toe.

I hardly noticed. In that few seconds, while I was sailing through the air, I'd spotted a long splinter of wood sticking out of the top of the new fence. Stuck to it were a scrap of the Lying Postman's uniform and a tuft of Red's hair.

The last piece of the puzzle had fallen into place, and I'd solved The Case of the Lying Postman.

Now all I had to do was to get Sarge to see the evidence.

In a **pawfect** world, I could have pointed my super-sniffer at the evidence. In a pawfect world, Sarge would have noticed it right away and made an arrest. Doggeroo is a doggedly good place, but it isn't pawfect. So what really happened was this.

1. Sarge ordered me to come out of

Ralf Boxer's garden.

2. I jack-yapped and jack-jumped as close to the evidence as I could.

3. Every time Sarge tried to grab me, I jack-jumped back.

4. Finally, Sarge had to lean right over the fence.

You can guess what happened next.

"Ouch!" yelled Sarge. He shot back from the fence, leaving a piece of *his* jacket on the splinter.

That's when Sarge noticed the piece of the Lying Postman's uniform already there. He picked it off and held it up to Ranger Jack and the Lying Postman.

"Could *that* be what bit you, do you think?" he asked, pointing at the splinter.

Of paws, the Lying Postman tried to

lie, but the evidence was there.

"There was a dog, too. I'm *sure* there was a dog," he said.

Sarge bent over the fence again, and picked up Ralf Boxer. "This one, maybe?" he asked, and held Ralf Boxer up close to the Lying Postman.

Ralf Boxer growled and snapped at the Lying Postman's nose.

Ranger Jack laughed.

The Lying Postman called Ralf Boxer something terrier-able, and marched away. We never saw him again.

Ralf Boxer believes he scared the Lying Postman away from Doggeroo. I know better. It was my brilliant detective work that really made him leave.

That was the end of The Case of the Lying Postman. Sarge took me home,

and on the way we met Kitty Booker,
with a yowling basket under her arm.

Fat Molly was going home.

"Scat, fat cat!" I yapped, and Fat Molly
said something really rude in Cat.

"Well, Foxie," I said, when we got

together later in the afternoon, "are you still ig-gnawing me?"

Foxie ig-gnawed me.

Just then, Lord Red came tearing up the street. "Jack, Jack, my poor gnawed paw is well again! Caterina Smith made it better and gave me a whole pile of beef bones! Are you coming to Uptown House to help me hide them, Jack? Are you?"

"Why not?" I said.

I left the yard (never mind how) and trotted off with Red.

As we were turning the corner, Foxie tore past us and vanished in a cloud of dust.

After that, I had a new challenge. How could Red and I hide the bones before Foxie stole them all?

Jack's Glossary

Jack-straction. *Distraction, done by a Jack.*

Pawfect. *Perfect, but about dogs. If it was cats, it would be "purrfect."*

About the Authors

Darrel and Sally Odgers live in Tasmania with their Jack Russell terriers, Tess, Trump, Pipwen, Jeanie and Preacher, who compete to take them for walks. They enjoy walks, because that's when they plan their stories. They toss ideas around and pick the best. They are also the authors of the popular *Pet Vet* series.

PET VET The new series from the authors of Jack Russell: Dog Detective!

Meet Trump! She's an A.L.O., or Animal Liaison Officer. She works with Dr. Jeanie, the young vet who runs Pet Vet Clinic in the country town of Cowfork. Dr. Jeanie looks after animals that are sick or injured. She also explains things to the owners. But what about the animals? Who will tell them what's going on? That's where Trump comes in.

JACK RUSSELL:
Dog Detective

Read all of Jack's adventures!

Jack Russell:
the detective with
a nose for crime.